THE FURRY FREEDOM FIGHTERS
THE ATTAC
GIANT
HOUND
TWO BOOKS IN ONE!
ALL HAIL THE JELLYFIEND!

Written by Nick Page
Illustrated by Tim Hutchinson
Designed by Jane Horne

Copyright © 2011 make believe ideas ltd
The Wilderness, Berkhamsted, Herts, HP4 2AZ.
565 Royal Parkway, Nashville, TN 37214, USA.
Text copyright © 2011 Nick Page

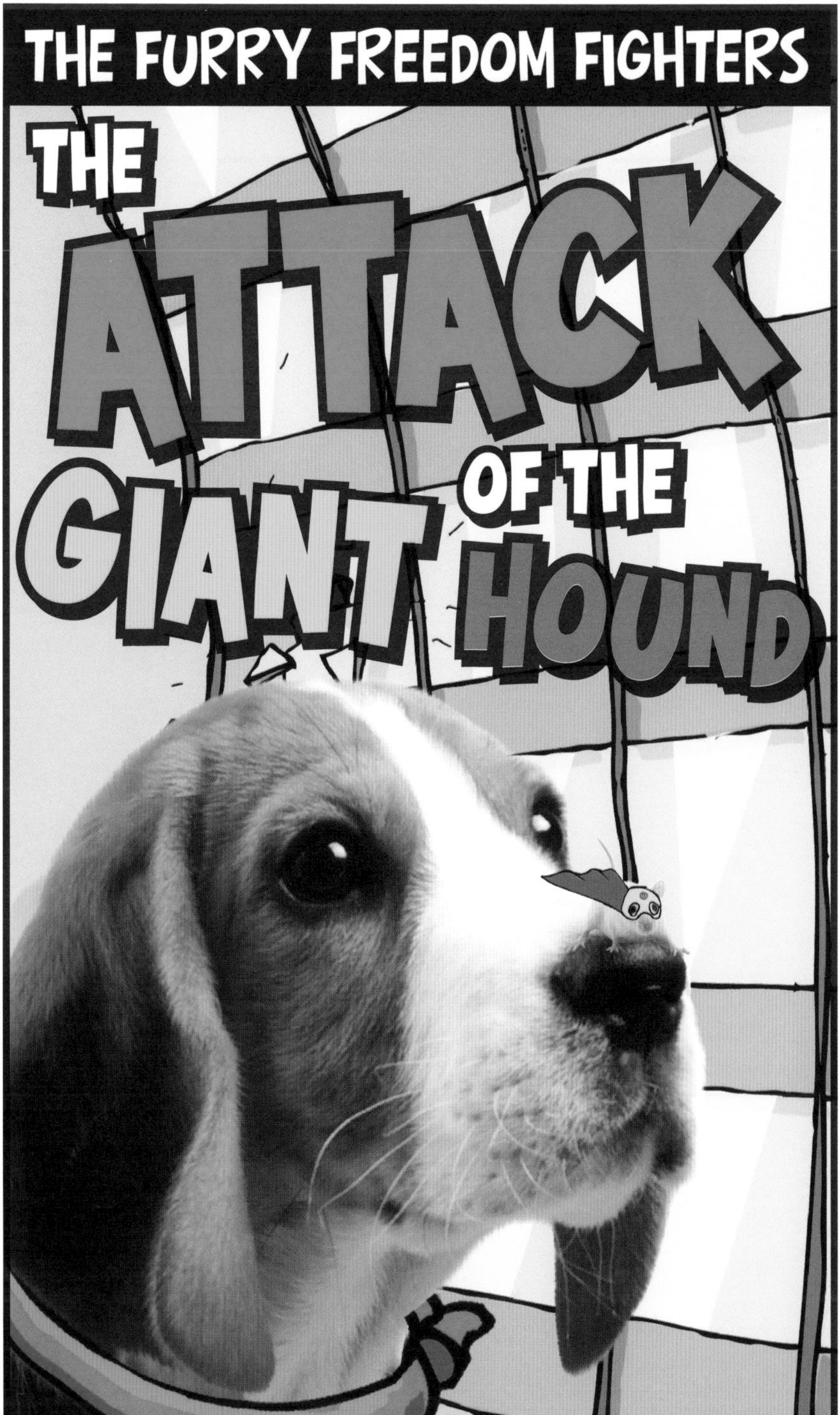
THE FURRY FREEDOM FIGHTERS
THE ATTACK OF THE GIANT HOUND

AT A SMALL, QUIET FARM IN NEW HAMSTERSHIRE JUST OUTSIDE THE CITY OF PETSHOPOLIS, EVERYTHING LOOKS NORMAL.
COME ON, BOY! LET'S GO FOR A WALK IN THE WOODS!
WOOF! WOOF!

IN THE WOODS...

GO ON, BOY! FETCH THE BALL!

BUT THEN THE BALL BOUNCES AWAY...

WAIT, BOY! WAIT FOR ME!

DOWN THE HILL THE BALL ROLLS, FOLLOWED CLOSELY BY THE PUPPY. FINALLY, THE BALL LANDS IN A STRANGE, GREEN POOL.

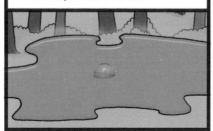

REACHING FOR THE BALL, THE PUPPY DIPS HIS HEAD INTO THE POOL...

WOOF!

MEANWHILE, AT "THE PERCH," THE HEADQUARTERS OF THE **FURRY FREEDOM FIGHTERS**...

WE FIND SUPERHAMMY, THE SUPER-POWERED HAMSTER, BUSY WORKING OUT — WHAT STRENGTH!

AND THERE IS MICROMOUSE, THE SUPER-SPEEDY, SIZE-SHRINKING SUPER-MOUSE — WHAT SPEED!

AND DON'T FORGET TURBO TORTOISE, THE RACING REPTILE, WHO IS ABOUT TO FIRE HIS NEW WATER CANNON — WHAT POWER!

SPLAAAASH!

AAAAARGH!

TOO MUCH POWER IN FACT, BECAUSE HE'S BLOWN HIMSELF THROUGH THE WALL.

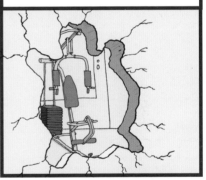

MAYBE I SHOULD HAVE PUT THE BRAKES ON FIRST.

I NEVER SAID I WANTED A SHOWER!

THE DOG SHAKES HIS HEAD AND POOR SUPERHAMMY FLIES OFF INTO A NEARBY RIVER.

WHILE THE FFF ARE FIGHTING THE HUGE HOUND, BACK AT THE PERCH BIRDBRAIN RECEIVES A MESSAGE FROM THE ARMY.

NOW HEAR THIS! YOU MUST **STOP** THAT DOG! HE IS HEADING TOWARDS THE HEART OF PETSHOPOLIS. IF YOU CAN'T STOP HIM, I'M GOING TO SEND IN THE BOMBERS!

BUT... THAT WILL DESTROY THE CITY!

THEN YOU'D BETTER STOP THAT DOG!

THAT'S VERY STRANGE!

SUDDENLY, BIRDBRAIN HAS A BRAINWAVE... BUT BEFORE OUR BRILLIANT BIRD BUDDY CAN DO ANYTHING...

ARE YOU READY, MICROMOUSE? WE NEED YOU TO DELIVER THOSE SLEEPING DROPS.

I CAN DO IT! TIME TO GO TO MICRO-SIZE!

USING HIS AMAZING MICRO-POWER, MICROMOUSE SHRINKS TO A TINY SIZE.

ZAP!

THEY CAN'T STOP ME IF THEY CAN'T SEE ME!

BUT THEN...

WOOF!

WOOF!

OH, NO! THE DOG'S BARK HAS BLOWN TURBO TORTOISE TO THE GROUND.

THIS HAS NOT BEEN A GOOD DAY.

SUDDENLY, SUPERHAMMY SEES SOMETHING IN THE SKY. BUT WHAT IS IT? INSECTS? MORE GIANT FLEAS? NO ... IT LOOKS LIKE PLANES!

THINK, SUPERHAMMY, THINK! THE PLANES ARE GETTING CLOSER! THEY COULD DESTROY PETSHOPOLIS!

AT THE SPEED OF SOUND, SUPERHAMMY FLIES INTO A NEARBY PARK AND PULLS OUT A TREE!

HERE, BOY! FETCH!

COME ON, BOY, CHASE THE STICK!

IT'S WORKING! THE GIANT PUPPY CHASES THE STICK, OR SHOULD WE SAY, THE TREE!

AND AS THE PUPPY STARTS TO LEAVE PETSHOPOLIS, SOMETHING BEGINS TO HAPPEN.

HE'S SHRINKING!

YOU FOUND HIM, SUPERHAMMY! WHERE HAVE YOU BEEN, BOY?

YOU WOULDN'T BELIEVE ME IF I TOLD YOU!

THE BIZARRE BEGINNINGS OF
BIRDBRAIN
GET HIM!
HE'S ESCAPING!
HE MUSTN'T TELL THE WORLD ABOUT THE KINGDOM OF THE BIRDS!
ARE YOU READY FOR THE AMAZING STORY OF THE WORLD'S BRAINIEST BIRD?

IN A COUNTRY FAR, FAR AWAY, THERE IS A MOUNTAIN. AND ON THAT MOUNTAIN THERE IS A CLIFF THAT NO MAN HAS EVER CLIMBED.

IT IS IMPOSSIBLE TO REACH.

TO GET THERE YOU HAVE TO FLY. AND THAT IS WHY IT IS CALLED...

THE KINGDOM OF THE BIRDS!

FOR THOUSANDS OF YEARS THIS PLACE HAS BEEN A SECRET. NOT MANY HUMANS KNOW THIS, BUT THERE ARE DIFFERENT KINDS OF BIRDS. MOST BIRDS ARE WILD, THEY SIMPLY FLY AROUND.

SOME BIRDS HAVE EVEN LEARNED HOW TO COPY HUMAN SPEECH.

WHO'S A PRETTY BOY, THEN?

BUT THERE ARE SOME BIRDS, LIKE ME, WHO HAVE SUPER-HUMAN INTELLIGENCE. AND WE ARE ALLOWED TO LIVE HERE, IN THE KINGDOM OF THE BIRDS!

REMEMBER, MY BROTHERS AND SISTERS: WE MUST ALWAYS KEEP THIS PLACE A SECRET. NO HUMAN MUST EVER BE ALLOWED TO FIND OUT ABOUT IT.

BUT WHAT'S THIS? THE KING OF THE BIRDS HASN'T SEEN THAT ONE MAN HAS DONE WHAT NO MAN HAS DONE BEFORE AND CLIMBED TO THE KINGDOM OF THE BIRDS!

AMAZING! THESE BIRDS CAN TALK! THEY CAN THINK!

BUT THE BIRDS HAVE NOTICED!

THEY DRIVE THE MAN FROM THE LEDGE, MAKING HIM FALL.

WE ARE DISCOVERED!

PUSH HIM OFF!

AAAAARGH!

BUT THE YOUNGEST BIRD IN THE KINGDOM, KNOWN AS BIRDBRAIN*, WANTS TO HELP THE MAN.

WE CAN'T LEAVE HIM TO DIE! WE MUST GET HIM HELP.

*WE COULD TELL YOU HIS REAL NAME, BUT IT IS IN THE LANGUAGE OF THE BIRDS SO YOU WOULDN'T UNDERSTAND IT.

YOU ARE FORBIDDEN TO HELP HIM! WE MUST LEAVE HIM TO DIE. HE KNOWS OUR SECRET!

BUT BIRDBRAIN DISOBEYS HIS KING AND FLIES OVER THE LEDGE!

I'VE HEARD ABOUT THESE! IT'S A SATELLITE PHONE. I CAN USE IT TO CALL FOR HELP!

AND SO BIRDBRAIN USES THE PHONE TO RESCUE THE MAN. BUT WHEN BIRDBRAIN RETURNS TO THE OTHERS...

YOU HAVE BROKEN THE RULES OF THE KINGDOM OF THE BIRDS. YOU MUST DIE!

BUT I ONLY DID WHAT WAS RIGHT!

DESTROY HIM, MY BIRDS! HE MUST DIE FOR HIS BETRAYAL!

THE BIRDS ATTACK, AND BIRDBRAIN FLIES FOR HIS LIFE!

I'M FREE! I MADE IT! I ESCAPED THEM THROUGH THE JUNGLE!

BUT HIS TINY BIRD HEART IS HEAVY.

I MAY BE FREE, BUT **I CAN NEVER GO BACK HOME!**

SO FOR MANY YEARS HE KEPT TRAVELING, LISTENING, AND LEARNING, UNTIL HE BECAME THE SUPER-INTELLIGENT CREATURE WE KNOW AS **BIRDBRAIN!**

FINALLY, HIS TRAVELS BROUGHT HIM TO THE CITY KNOWN AS PETSHOPOLIS...

THIS CITY IS SO DANGEROUS AND SO SAD. THESE HUMANS NEED HELP FROM US ANIMALS. I SHALL USE MY BRAIN TO HELP THEM.

SO HE SET UP THE PERCH, HIS SECRET LABORATORY. AND THEN ONE DAY HE HAD AN IDEA...

THERE MUST BE OTHER ANIMALS WITH SPECIAL ABILITIES. WE COULD FORM A TEAM. NO, A SUPER-TEAM!

AND SO BEGAN **THE FURRY FREEDOM FIGHTERS!** ALL BECAUSE OF THE BRAVE AND BRAINY BIRD: **BIRDBRAIN!**

THE END...
(NEARLY)

PETSHOPOLIS, HOME OF THE **FURRY FREEDOM FIGHTERS,** A SUPER-TEAM READY TO PROTECT THE CITY FROM ALL ITS ENEMIES.

BUT PETSHOPOLIS IS JUST ONE CITY IN ONE COUNTRY...

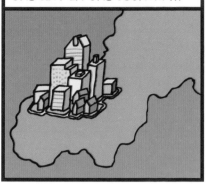

WHICH IS JUST ONE COUNTRY OF MANY ON THE PLANET WE CALL EARTH...

WHICH IS JUST ONE PLANET OF MANY THOUSANDS IN THE UNIVERSE...

MEANWHILE, BACK IN PETSHOPOLIS, SOME CRIMINAL CATS ARE STEALING ALL OF THE CITY'S FISH!

SUPERHAMMY HAS GRABBED THE CATS' GETAWAY CAR!

THE CRAZY CATS GO FOR THEIR GUNS!

BUT THEN...

THIS ISN'T MY GUN, IT'S A BANANA!

I'VE GOT A BANANA AS WELL!

ME, TOO. AND THIS ONE IS ALL ROTTEN!

YOU SHOULD KNOW BETTER! GUNS ARE DANGEROUS. THAT'S WHY I USED MY SUPER MICRO-SPEED TO TAKE THEM AND REPLACE THEM WITH BANANAS. BANANAS ARE GOOD FOR YOU!

RUN FOR IT!

THE CATS START TO RUN AWAY. THEN SUDDENLY...

SUDDENLY, MICROMOUSE FALLS TO THE GROUND!

MICROMOUSE! WHAT'S WRONG?

HE'S ILL. WE HAVE TO GET HIM BACK TO THE PERCH!

SUPERHAMMY AND TURBO TORTOISE FLY MICROMOUSE BACK TO THE PERCH, THE HEADQUARTERS OF THE FURRY FREEDOM FIGHTERS.

WHAT'S THE MATTER? WHAT'S WRONG WITH HIM?

WHAT'S THAT?

I'M NOT SURE, BUT I THINK HE HAS A RARE CASE OF **FISHNANA DISEASE!**

HOW DID HE CATCH IT? WILL HE BE ALRIGHT?

WAIT A MINUTE! WHAT'S THAT STRANGE LIGHT?

FISH CATCH IT BY EATING ROTTEN BANANAS. HE MUST HAVE CAUGHT IT FROM THOSE CATS! WHEN FISH CATCH IT, THEY SNEEZE TO DEATH, BUT SINCE HE'S A MOUSE, I THINK HE'LL BE OK.

WITH HIS SUPER-HAMSTER STRENGTH, SUPERHAMMY PREPARES TO ATTACK. BUT THEN...

ZAAAAAAAAP

UH-OH...
I DON'T FEEL
TOO GOOD.

UGHHH.

WELL?
ARE YOU GOING
TO ATTACK?

I WILL
OBEY...

OH, NO! WHAT'S HAPPENED
TO SUPERHAMMY?

TURBO TORTOISE FOLLOWS HIS HYPNOTIZED FRIENDS DOWN ONTO THE STREET, WHERE A SHOCK IS WAITING FOR HIM!

MADE IT! AND I'VE GOT AN IDEA!

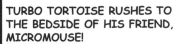

TURBO TORTOISE RUSHES TO THE BEDSIDE OF HIS FRIEND, MICROMOUSE!

WHAT'S HAPPENING?

SORRY, OLD FRIEND, I NEED YOUR HELP!

WHAT'S THIS? TURBO TORTOISE HAS TAKEN MICROMOUSE UP TO THE ROOF AND LOADED HIM INTO HIS TURBO CATAPULT.

LEAVE ME ALONE! I'M NOT FEELING WELL.

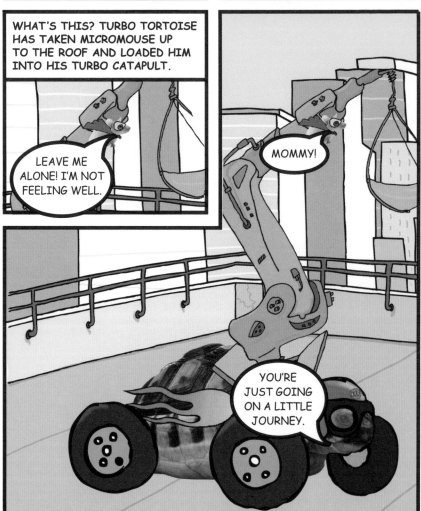

MOMMY!

YOU'RE JUST GOING ON A LITTLE JOURNEY.

THE JELLYFIEND SNEEZES AND EXPLODES INTO MULTICOLORED GLOOP!

AND DOWN ON THE STREET EVERYONE STARTS TO WAKE UP.

AND SO ANOTHER CASE HAS ENDED AND THE WORLD IS SAFE AGAIN THANKS TO THE **FURRY FREEDOM FIGHTERS!**

SO, MY FRIEND, YOU THOUGHT YOU COULD SPY ON ME! BUT I CAUGHT YOU, AND NOW YOU WILL BE MY FINEST EXPERIMENT!

IS THAT TURBO TORTOISE? NO, NOT YET, READER. AS OUR STORY BEGINS, HE IS JUST PLAIN TERRY TORTOISE, THE GOVERNMENT AGENT.

THE GOVERNMENT KNOW WHAT YOU ARE DOING, YOU FIEND. AND THEY WILL STOP YOU!

OH, I DON'T THINK SO. I HAVE TURNED YOU INTO **A WALKING TIME BOMB!** AND I WILL CONTROL YOU USING THIS REMOTE CONTROL!

YOU'RE NUTS!

NO, I AM DR. NUTTY!

NOW, IT'S TIME TO GET STARTED. DON'T WORRY, NO ONE WILL NOTICE YOU IN THAT ROCK DISGUISE! YOU ARE NOW COMPLETELY CONTROLLED BY ME. AND YOU ARE WALKING TO YOUR DOOM!

I ... I CAN'T STOP WALKING!

TICK! TOCK! TICK! TOCK!

HE'S TURNED ME INTO SOME KIND OF ROBOT. BUT ALL I HAVE TO DO IS WARN THE PEOPLE OF PETSHOPOLIS.

BUT WHEN TERRY TRIES TO SPEAK...

I CAN'T TALK! I CAN'T SAY ANYTHING!

DID YOU THINK I WOULD MAKE IT EASY? I'VE CREATED A SPECIAL CONTROL TO STOP YOU FROM SPEAKING!

AND SO, TERRY TORTOISE BEGINS THE TERRIBLE TREK TO HIS **DOOM!**

BUT ALL IS NOT LOST, FOR HIGH ABOVE THE CITY THERE FLIES ANOTHER HERO — THE BRAINY BIRD KNOWN AS BIRDBRAIN!

THAT'S ODD! WHAT'S HAPPENING DOWN THERE? I'D BETTER HAVE A LOOK.

YOU JUST STOPPED!

I HAD TO! THIS NUTTY ROCK JUST WALKED OUT IN FRONT OF ME!

BIRDBRAIN FLIES ON AND THEN HE DISCOVERS SOMETHING ELSE.

WHAT HAPPENED HERE?

THIS WALKING ROCK JUST WALKED STRAIGHT THROUGH MY FRUIT STAND!

AND WHAT'S HAPPENED HERE? IT LOOKS LIKE SOMETHING HAS JUST GONE STRAIGHT THROUGH!

NOT SOMETHING, BIRDBRAIN, **SOMEONE:** TERRY TORTOISE UNDER THE CONTROL OF DR. NUTTY!

I CAN'T TELL HIM! I CAN'T MAKE A SOUND!

WHAT'S UP, FRIEND? ARE YOU OK? CAN YOU SPEAK?

BUT THEN...

WAIT, WHAT'S THIS? IT'S A CONTROL TO STOP YOU FROM SPEAKING!

QUICKLY, BIRDBRAIN REMOVES THE CONTROL.

THANK YOU! I CAN SPEAK! YOU HAVE TO STOP ME! THERE'S A BOMB IN MY SHELL AND IT WILL GO OFF!

LET ME LOOK! I CAN HELP!

WITHIN SECONDS THE BRAINY BIRD HAS SPOTTED THE BIG BOMB!

I CAN STOP THIS!

THERE'S NO TIME! GET THE ARMY TO DUMP ME IN THE SEA!

TICK!

TOCK!

NO! I CAN SAVE YOU!

FLY AWAY! SAVE YOURSELF!

BIRDBRAIN WORKS AS FAST AS HE CAN, BUT...

KAA-BOOM!

OH, NO! IS HE TOO LATE?

AND SO TERRY TORTOISE BECAME TURBO TORTOISE, AND HE JOINED YOUR FAVORITES: **THE FURRY FREEDOM FIGHTERS!**

WHO'S THE FASTEST? WHO'S THE STRONGEST? WHO'S THE MOST EVIL?

FIND OUT MORE ABOUT
THE FURRY FREEDOM FIGHTERS
AND THEIR FEARSOME FOES!

BIRDBRAIN

BIRDBRAIN COMES FROM THE MYSTERIOUS KINGDOM OF THE BIRDS. NOT JUST A FAMOUS INVENTOR, HE IS ALSO THE BRAINS BEHIND THE FURRY FREEDOM FIGHTERS.

REAL NAME: TOO HARD TO PRONOUNCE!

BRAINS: ★★★★★

STRENGTH: ★

SPEED: ★★

WEAPONS: ★★★

SURPRISE: ★★★

WEAKNESS: HE MAY BE BRAINY, BUT HE'S JUST A BIRD, SO HE CAN BE OVERPOWERED BY STRONG ENEMIES.

MICROMOUSE

WHILE ESCAPING FROM A SECRET LABORATORY, MICROMOUSE WAS HIT BY A SHRINKING RAY, GIVING HIM THE ABILITY TO TURN SUPER-SMALL AND GO SUPER-FAST!

REAL NAME: UNKNOWN

BRAINS: ★★

STRENGTH: ★

SPEED: ★★★★★

WEAPONS: ★

SURPRISE: ★★★★★

WEAKNESS: CHEESE — HE CAN'T RESIST IT! AND WHEN HE IS MICRO-SIZE, HE ALWAYS RUNS THE RISK OF BEING STEPPED ON.

TURBO TORTOISE

SECRET GOVERNMENT AGENT, TERRY TORTOISE, WAS TURNED INTO A WALKING TIME BOMB BY THE EVIL SQUIRREL, DR. NUTTY!

REAL NAME: TERRY TORTOISE

BRAINS: ★★★

STRENGTH: ★★★★★

SPEED: ★★★★

WEAPONS: ★★★★★

SURPRISE: ★★★

WEAKNESS: BEING TIPPIED OVER! LIKE ALL TORTOISES, IF YOU TIP HIM OVER, HE HAS PROBLEMS GETTING UP AGAIN!

SUPERHAMMY

SUPERHAMMY IS THE SUPER-POWERED HAMSTER.
HE CAN FLY THROUGH THE AIR, HE CAN TEAR UP WHOLE
TREES — WHAT MORE COULD YOU WANT FROM A HAMSTER?

REAL NAME: HAMMY THE HAMSTER

BRAINS: ★★★

STRENGTH: ★★★★★

SPEED: ★★★★

WEAPONS: ★

SURPRISE: ★★

WEAKNESS: BEING A HAMSTER, SUPERHAMMY'S
BIGGEST CHALLENGE IS STAYING
AWAKE DURING THE DAY!

THE CAT-NAP GANG

THIS GANG OF FELINE THIEVES IS ALWAYS TRYING TO STEAL THINGS IN PETSHOPOLIS — AND THEY ALWAYS GET CAUGHT BY THE FURRY FREEDOM FIGHTERS!

REAL NAME: TEDDY, EDDY, AND FREDDIE.

BRAINS: ★

STRENGTH: ★★★

SPEED: ★★★

WEAPONS: ★

SURPRISE: ★★★

WEAKNESS: THEY THINK THAT THEY CAN ALWAYS GET AWAY WITH IT!

THE GIANT HOUND

IS HE A FRIEND OR A FOE? THIS GIANT PUPPY TERRORIZED PETSHOPOLIS AFTER STEPPING IN A VERY PECULIAR PUDDLE!

REAL NAME: DOGZILLA

BRAINS: ★

STRENGTH: ★★★★★

SPEED: ★★

WEAPONS: ★

SURPRISE: ★

WEAKNESS: LOVES CHASING THINGS! (BUT YOU HAVE TO BE PRETTY STRONG TO THROW THEM — HE'S SO BIG YOU HAVE TO THROW A TREE!)

THE JELLYFIEND

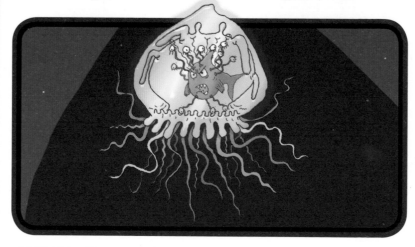

THE MYSTERIOUS JELLYFIEND CAME FROM OUTER SPACE.
HE IS A MULTICOLORED, GLOOP-FILLED JELLYFISH.
AND THAT'S ALL WE KNOW!

REAL NAME: WHO KNOWS?

BRAINS: ★★★★★

STRENGTH: ★★

SPEED: ★

WEAPONS: ★★★★★

SURPRISE: ★★★★

WEAKNESS: LET'S JUST SAY THAT IF HE CATCHES
A COLD, YOU SHOULD BE CAREFUL!

MORE AMAZING ADVENTURES FROM THE FURRY FREEDOM FIGHTERS:

FFF **FURRY FREEDOM FIGHTERS**

THE DAWN OF THE RED FANG

THE FURRY FREEDOM FIGHTERS NEVER LEAVE AN ANIMAL BEHIND

OF DR. K

OUT NOW!